PIECE BY PIECE!

Mosaics of the Ancient World

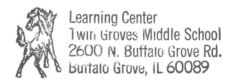

PIECE BY PIECE!

Mosaics of the Ancient World

by Michael Avi-Yonah

Runestone Press • Minneapolis

RUNESTONE PRESS • RUNESTONE

rune (rōon) *n* **1 a :** one of the earliest written alphabets used in northern Europe, dating back to A.D. 200; **b :** an alphabet character believed to have magic powers; **c :** a charm; **d :** an Old Norse or Finnish poem. **2 :** a poem or incantation of mysterious significance, often carved in stone.

Thanks to Dr. Guy Gibbon, Department of Anthropology, University of Minnesota, for his help in preparing this book.

Words in **bold** type are listed in a glossary on page 61.

Library of Congress Cataloging-in-Publication Data
Avi-Yonah, Michael
    Piece by piece!: mosaics of the ancient world / by Michael Avi-Yonah.
        p. cm — (Buried Worlds)
    Includes index.
    Summary: Describes ancient and modern mosaic techniques, as well as early Greek, Roman, and Byzantine mosaics.
    ISBN 0-8225-3204-2 (lib. bdg.)
    1. Mosaics, Ancient—Juvenile literature. 2. Mosaics, Greek—Juvenile literature. 3. Mosaics, Roman—Juvenile literature. [1. Mosaics.]
I. Title. II. Series.
NA3760.A82 1993
738.5'2'0938—dc20   93-10746
                                                                CIP
                                                                AC

Manufactured in the United States of America
1 2 3 4 5 6 – I/JR – 98 97 96 95 94 93

CONTENTS

THE ART OF MOSAICS

Mosaics are pictures or patterns made with small pieces of colored material held together with **cement.** The pieces—called **tesserae**—may consist of bits of stone, tiles made of baked clay, or squares of glass. Some tesserae are as large as playing cards, while others are as small as match tips. **Archaeologists** (scientists who find and study ancient objects) have uncovered mosaics that are as much as 5,000 years old.

Ancient mosaicists (mosaic artists) made pictures in many shapes and sizes. Their works decorated furniture or the handles of tools or weapons. Other mosaics covered the walls, floors, or ceilings of large buildings.

Some ancient mosaics contained a variety of hues. Others had few colors or were made only of black and white pieces. This wide range of sizes, shapes, and colors allowed ancient artists to create unique mosaics in many styles.

From Floor to Ceiling

Most artwork created in ancient times was made of materials that quickly rotted. Paintings on canvas and wood, for example, survived only if they were kept clean and dry. Mosaics, on the other hand, are nearly indestructible, since most cement and tesserae materials do not decay and are not easily worn down.

Ancient mosaic artists often used brightly colored tesserae (mosaic pieces) to create geometric patterns or pictures of people and animals.

Pavements—mosaics cemented into a floor—are particularly solid, and many ancient pavements are well preserved. When old buildings collapsed, their walls caved in, burying the mosaic pavements under piles of rubble. Centuries later, archaeologists carefully unearthed and restored many buried pavements.

The ancient Roman architect Vitruvius described in his writings how early mosaic artists prepared the foundation of a pavement. After leveling the ground, workers laid a thick bottom layer of rough pebbles on which was spread a second layer of cement and smashed bricks. The final and most important layer consisted of cement and

A mosaic depicting a watch dog guards this entrance to an ancient dwelling in Pompeii, Italy. Archaeologists—scientists who dig up and study ancient artifacts— believe the pavement (floor mosaic) served as a warning to intruders.

Ancient mosaicists (mosaic artists) strengthened floor mosaics with underlays of cement and ground bricks. Most pavements were made to withstand constant use.

finely ground bricks. Artists used this mixture to hold the tesserae in place.

Ancient mosaicists made most pavements with different kinds of natural stone, which could bear heavy foot traffic without destroying the design. Natural stones come in a variety of colors. Marble, for example, exists in shades of yellow, green, red, and white.

There were several methods for making ancient mosaic pavements. Some artists created the entire mosaic inside the building where it was to remain. Using this method, the mosaicist first drew a rough design on the second layer. The artist prepared fresh cement and spread it over a small area of the rough sketch. Piece by piece, the mosaicist carefully pressed the tesserae into the wet mixture.

When the picture was completed, the artist made a border of tesserae—usually of a single color—around the design, leaving the background blank. The artist's assistants often filled in the background using the border color.

Some mosaic artists prepared their pictures in special workshops that were located away from the pavement site. After workers laid a background of tesserae at the site, the pictures were brought in from the workshop and inserted in large spaces left open for the main design.

Scholars believe that a third mosaic method existed. Instead of

An artist employs a hammer (above) to crush natural stone into mosaic pieces. Mortar (below)— a cement mixture— holds the tesserae together.

pressing the pieces directly into the wet cement, some mosaicists glued the tesserae on a design that was drawn on paper or canvas. Because pavements were large, the design was probably attached to a backing in sections.

After the preliminary work was finished, the sections arrived at the pavement site. The artist pressed the exposed surfaces into the wet cement and then peeled off the backing to reveal a mosaic picture. To complete the mosaic, the artist filled in gaps between the tesserae with cement and polished the mosaic's surface.

Most wall mosaics, which did not need to withstand foot traffic, had more complex designs than pavements did. The tesserae were usually smaller—often less than one-fourth of an inch (one-half centimeter) in width—allowing the mosaicist to use more pieces and to create greater detail.

The base of a wall mosaic was made of the same materials as the base of a pavement. The main goal in building a wall base was to prevent individual tesserae or patches of tesserae and cement from coming loose. For this reason, workers allowed each layer to harden and

A modern mosaicist carefully pieces together a picture with natural stones.

Wall mosaics survive among the remains of an ancient building in Herculaneum, Italy. These pictures were preserved under tons of lava and volcanic ash, which buried the cities of Herculaneum and nearby Pompeii during the eruption of Mount Vesuvius in A.D. 79.

then moistened it again before applying the next layer. The moisture created a strong bond between the base layers. Artists then slowly and carefully applied the tesserae and cement to craft the final artwork.

On the Surface

When viewed from a distance, the individual colored pieces of a mosaic blend together to form a picture. Similar colors placed next to one another, however, sometimes blend too well and blur the outlines and contours of a mosaic.

To solve this problem, ancient artists used contrasting colors that at close range often appeared to clash but seemed natural from far away. For example, the shadows in the folds of a red dress might have been colored blue or even dark green to create a distinct contrast. A shadow on a blue mountain might be made of purple rather than of darker blue tesserae.

Ancient mosaicists made durable pavements primarily of stone. When crafting wall mosaics artists were free to use more delicate materials. A frequently used substance for ancient wall mosaics was glass—a hard, clear material composed of sand, lime, and soda.

An artist puts the finishing touches on an outdoor wall mosaic.

Mosaicists make glass tesserae by flattening colored glass into sheets (above) *and then cutting the material into small pieces* (right).

Soldiers from Mesopotamia (modern Iraq) march into battle on this panel, which dates to 2500 B.C. The picture, which is a forerunner to mosaic art, is made of bits of shell and lapis lazuli (a blue stone) set in wood.

Craftspeople heated this mineral mixture, formed it into cube-shaped tesserae, and allowed the cubes to harden.

Glass could be combined with other minerals and manufactured in a variety of bright colors, including red, yellow, green, blue, black, and white. Some ancient artists created gold tesserae by wrapping one side of a glass cube with gold foil and then covering the foil with a thin coating of clear glass that protected the color.

Artists paid close attention to any natural light that might strike glass

15

tesserae. They often set the glass pieces at different angles to allow the light reflected off the surface to scatter in many directions.

Wall mosaics may also have included bits of shell, baked clay, wood, and bone. Artists often combined these materials with more durable tesserae to create their artworks.

The First Mosaics

The oldest surviving mosaics were crafted in about 3000 B.C. in the ancient kingdom of Sumer in Mesopotamia (modern Iraq). Archaeologists have unearthed a Sumerian wall decorated with cone-shaped pegs. The pegs, which range from 1 to 2 inches long (2.5 to 5 cm),

TOOLS AND TESSERAE

The basic techniques of mosaic art have changed little since the fourth century B.C. Some modern artists duplicate the materials and techniques of ancient mosaicists to create works in a traditional style. Other artisans have broadened their array of tools and tesserae to make more contemporary images.

Traditional artists use tesserae of pressed glass, ceramic (baked clay), window glass, marble, or smalti (enamel). More daring mosaicists look for unusual mosaic materials, such as rocks, plastic, paper, or even uncooked pasta and dried vegetables.

Both traditional and modern mosaicists employ two different methods to hand-cut hard surfaces of stone and glass. The hutch and scaling hammer, which mosaicists have used since ancient times, make very accurate cuts. A hutch consists of a wide metal blade embedded in a sturdy wooden block. A mosaicist firmly holds the tesserae material on top of the blade and with a sharp, quick blow brings down the scaling hammer directly over the hutch blade. The blow cuts the material exactly where it meets the blade.

In recent times, cut nippers have become a popular mosaic tool. Resembling pliers (a hand tool for holding and twisting small objects), cut nippers are used like scissors. But this tool cannot easily clip very small tesserae. Other handy tools for mosaic making include flat-bladed putty knives and trowels for spreading cement, tweezers for picking up tiny pieces, and paintbrushes for cleaning and polishing the mosaic surface.

Mosaicists use cut nippers (left) *to shape tesserae and tweezers* (center) *to pick up very small pieces.*

17

were pressed into mud. The Sumerians colored the visible ends of the pegs black, red, and white.

Because these cones were not flat pieces, mosaicists do not consider them to be true tesserae. The earliest known examples of tesserae, which date to 2600 B.C., were found in the Sumerian city of Ur. At this site, archaeologists discovered drinking vessels and other small objects that were decorated with flat fragments of shell, bone, lapis lazuli (a blue stone), and red limestone set in pitch (a black, tar-like substance).

Eventually, ancient people began using pebbles to make pavements. These pebble designs represent a transition from simple mosaics to the large and elaborate mosaics of the ancient Greek, Roman, and Byzantine empires, which all thrived on or near the Mediterranean Sea.

Ancient artists pressed black, red, and white pegs into mud to create this wall. Archaeologists uncovered the wall, which dates to about 3000 B.C., in the Mesopotamian city of Uruk.

Crowds gather to view a Roman pavement unearthed in London, England, in 1869. Archaeologists have discovered ancient mosaics in many areas of the world, including the Middle East, the Mediterranean region, Africa, northern Europe, and the Americas.

MOSAICS OF ANCIENT GREECE

The Greeks began to make decorative mosaics in the fourth century B.C. Archaeologists have found excellent examples of early Greek mosaics in the ruins of ancient Olynthus. King Philip II of Macedonia destroyed this northern Greek city in 348 B.C. Since the city was not rebuilt, all of its remains must have been made on or before that date.

The artists of Olynthus used only two colors in their pebbled mosaics. This style imitated a popular type of Greek pottery that featured rust-colored figures on black backgrounds. This pottery was greatly admired by people throughout the Mediterranean and western Asia. Greek artists often made the back-grounds of their mosaics entirely of black, blue, green, or red pebbles. Figures appeared in light-colored pebbles of white or tan.

Archaeologists believe that these mosaic pavements had religious significance for the ancient people of Olynthus. Some pavements, for example, are decorated with symbols that inhabitants believed brought good luck or warded off evil. Other mosaics depict the gods and goddesses of ancient Greek mythology.

The Mosaics at Pella

Ancient mosaicists in Pella, the capital of Macedonia, created more detail in their work, which dates to about 300 B.C. Like the mosaics from Olynthus, the Pella mosaics were made of natural pebbles but were crafted in many different colors.

The Pella mosaicists bordered their works with designs of animals and leaves. Some of the figures and details were outlined in strips of lead, a grayish metal. Archaeologists believe that the artists at first used these strips as a working guide. The lead later became an important decorative element.

Although the Pella mosaics, like those in Olynthus, were generally made in two colors, some details were highlighted. Hair, for example, might have been colored in red or yellow.

One of the most famous mosaics at Pella depicts two hunters, with their cloaks blowing wildly in the wind, attacking a deer. One figure, whose hat has flown off, has seized the deer by the antlers and is preparing to stab it. The other hunter stands ready to kill the deer with a battle ax. A hunting dog is

Mosaicists in the ancient Greek city of Olynthus set white designs into backgrounds of black, blue, red, or green. Here, a warrior battles a mythological monster called a chimera, a beast with a lion's head, a goat's body, and a serpent's tail.

holding on to the deer as well. Surrounding the mosaic is a border of lilies and acanthus (a thorny plant). Although the artist cemented small pebbles into a flat surface to create the scene, the artist's skill makes the figures seem lifelike.

The Greeks crafted more elaborate pavements in the late fourth century B.C. Instead of simple pebbles, mosaicists began to use pieces of carefully cut stone, hardened clay, or colored glass. These new materials enabled artists to create finer detail. Although the more brilliant colors outshined the simple stones of the earlier mosaics, the basic technique of mosaic art remained unchanged.

Scenes of Egypt

During the fourth century B.C., when ancient Greece had great power and influence in the Mediterranean region, the Greeks established cities in many locations

Crafted of small pebbles, this pavement from the ancient Greek city of Pella shows a deer hunt within an intricate border of flowers and plants.

Many ancient Greek mosaics featured Egyptian locations. The Nile River flows past elaborate buildings and wild animals in this illustrated map of the Nile Valley.

beyond Greece's borders. One of the most important of these Greek cities was Alexandria, a Mediterranean port located in northern Africa near the mouth of the Nile River.

The Egyptians farmed along the fertile banks of the Nile and by about 2700 B.C. began to build great pyramids to protect the tombs of their pharaohs (rulers). Egyptian culture greatly impressed the Greek artists of Alexandria, who adopted many Egyptian scenes in their mosaics.

One of the earliest Alexandrian mosaics—an illustrated map of the Nile Valley—dates to the first century B.C. The mosaic shows the Nile River running through the valley from Sudan (a country south of Egypt) to the Mediterranean Sea.

The map depicts Greek villas (large homes), the arrival of boats, and a feast being held under a tent. Scenes of the countryside, an ancient temple, hunting, and Egyptian wildlife are also part of the mosaic's design. The artist chose dragons and other mythical beings to represent the unknown interior of Africa beyond Sudan.

Archaeologists have unearthed other mosaics that further reveal

Ducks swim among the lily pads of the Nile River in this ancient Greek mosaic.

the popularity of Egyptian subjects with Greek artists. An ancient mosaic in Alexandria itself depicts the city as a woman with wide-open eyes, wearing a ship on her head for a crown.

A Theatrical Review

Excavators have found other mosaic pavements by Greek artists in the ruins of the ancient town of Pompeii, in southern Italy. A sudden eruption of the nearby volcano Mount Vesuvius destroyed Pompeii in A.D. 79. The lava and ashes that buried Pompeii also preserved many examples of Greek art.

Archaeologists have been digging in the ruins of Pompeii for more than 200 years and have unearthed a treasure of ancient buildings, tools, writings, and artworks.

Discovered in Pompeii, this detail from an ancient Greek mosaic depicts a roving street musician beating a drum. Originally a Greek village, Pompeii contains many works of the early Greek mosaicists.

MAGNIFICENT FOES

In the fourth century B.C., the rulers of two powerful nations struggled for control of the Middle East. Alexander the Great ruled Macedonia, an area that included northern Greece and parts of southeastern Europe. To the east, King Darius governed Persia (modern Iran). In 333 B.C., the two leaders met in battle near the village of Gaugamela in modern Iraq. Inspired by this momentous conflict, an artist recreated the action on a mosaic pavement in Pompeii, Italy.

The left side of this elaborate battle scene shows a determined Alexander leading his mounted warriors. On the right is Darius, who stands in a chariot (a two-wheeled wagon). A Persian nobleman, who has thrown himself in front of Darius to protect the king, lies wounded by Alexander's spear. Darius reaches forward, attempting to help the loyal warrior.

Although the Persian forces far outnumbered Alexander's small army, the Macedonians' battle tactics were superior. Sensing defeat, the Persians in this mosaic signal for more troops, but help did not arrive in time to stop Alexander. Defeated, Darius fled the battlefield. Although parts of the pavement have crumbled with age, the picture has offered archaeologists a detailed portrayal of Alexander's great victory.

This pavement from Pompeii depicts a bloody battle between the ancient rulers Alexander the Great of Macedonia and Darius, the king of Persia (modern Iran).

A group of actors prepares for a performance in this Greek mosaic. The popularity of the theater greatly influenced Greek artists.

These discoveries have taught us a great deal about the everyday lives of the Greeks and Romans.

Although Pompeii was part of the Roman Empire, the city was originally a Greek town. Theatrical performances were very popular among the Greeks, who staged their plays in large, outdoor amphitheaters. Many Greek artists depicted theatrical scenes in mosaics at Pompeii.

One pavement shows a director distributing masks to a group of actors as they put on their costumes. Another depicts a scene from an ancient comedy, in which a young woman consults a phony fortune-teller. Instead of using a crystal ball, however, the fortune-teller gazes at a vase. A third mosaic portrays a scene of roving street musicians wearing masks. One musician beats a drum, another plays the castanets (a wooden finger instrument), and the third blows into a flute.

Mosaic Mirrors

Greek artists sometimes set mosaic pictures into small spaces surrounded by ornate mosaic designs. These elaborate decorations, which often covered an entire floor, copied patterns in the ceiling above. This method gave the illusion that the decorations on the ceiling were reflected on the floor, as if in a mirror.

Mosaicists often used the mirror effect in outdoor passageways roofed with **pergolas**—wooden frames covered with vines. Mosaic artists set pergola patterns into passageway floors to mirror the real vines overhead. Archaeologists have discovered numerous pergola mosaics crafted by the ancient Greeks.

Excavators found this mosaic of an actor's mask among the ruins of Pompeii. The Greeks, who enjoyed drama, used masks to portray the personality or emotions of a stage character.

MOSAICS OF THE ROMAN EMPIRE

During the first and second centuries A.D., the power and influence of Rome grew steadily. Most of Europe and the lands bordering the Mediterranean Sea became part of one vast empire controlled by the Romans. The mosaic art that had developed in Greece spread to Rome. From there, mosaics soon appeared in all corners of the Roman Empire, from England in the west to Syria in the east, and from Germany in the north to Libya in the south.

African Mosaics

Archaeologists have uncovered thousands of mosaics in the Roman provinces of North Africa, where this art form adorned the floors of villas, temples, bathhouses, and public buildings. These mosaics illustrate ancient mythology, sports, contests, and rural life.

Vivid and colorful, North African mosaics portray realistic and sometimes violent scenes. For example, a pavement in Libya depicts fighting between gladiators—Roman slaves or prisoners who battled to the death to entertain spectators. Every detail of these contests is portrayed, including musicians who signaled the start of the fights.

Another North African work portrays executions. Prisoners, who are bound to stakes, are mauled to

Archaeologists discovered many mosaics in northern Africa, including this geometric pattern (above) from Tunisia and a work that includes human forms (below) in Morocco.

This mosaic from Libya shows the execution of a prisoner by wild animals.

death by wild animals released by executioners. The mosaics found in North Africa are the most detailed representations of these violent punishments.

Mosaics of Ostia and Antioch

During the second century A.D., Roman mosaicists began to move away from the style of multi-colored, realistic pavements. Artisans experimented with black-and-white mosaics made of carefully prepared cubes.

Archaeologists have discovered some of the best examples of this style in Ostia, a seaport near Rome. Merchants throughout the Roman Empire brought their ships to Ostia. Many of the black-and-white mosaics in the seaport depict other harbors in the empire, as well as ships and sailors.

Many of the mosaics found at Ostia also portray fanciful scenes of maritime mythology. For instance, one work shows Neptune, the Roman god of the sea, driving a chariot (a two-wheeled battle cart) drawn by fish-tailed horses. A number of animals and mythological creatures, all of which are half-fish, surround Neptune.

Roman mosaic art also developed in the eastern part of the empire. In Antioch, a site in modern Turkey, archaeologists have traced a progression of mosaic styles. Older mosaic pavements at Antioch consisted of many individual pictures, each surrounded by an elaborate border. The area devoted to the single pictures gradually increased until it covered the entire surface of a pavement and included almost no border.

Mosaicists in the ancient Roman seaport of Ostia used carefully shaped cubes to create their distinct black-and-white mosaics. This picture depicts a sailor loading goods on a trading ship.

Most of the mosaics discovered at Antioch depict gods and other characters from Greek and Roman mythology, especially Dionysus, the Greek god of wine. Mosaics of Dionysus appear most often in banquet halls, where guests could admire the artwork as they feasted.

Roman Decline

About A.D. 200, the Roman Empire began to experience political and economic problems that eventually led to its decline. By A.D. 300, these problems had become very serious. The people of the late

Inspired by the nearby Mediterranean Sea, many Roman mosaicists created works associated with the ocean, such as this colorful portrayal of sea life.

This detailed Roman mosaic of a lion and her cub dates to the fourth century A.D.

Roman Empire longed for a simple and peaceful life. Thus, many mosaicists of the time began to express religious and philosophical ideas that gave people hope.

For example, many works depicted the yearly cycle of the seasons, which encouraged the belief that the hard times of winter would pass and the good times of spring and summer would return again. Other mosaics express themes of security, tranquility, generosity, and strength. The most common theme is hunger. From these mosaics, archaeologists have learned a great deal about the qual-ity of life in the Roman Empire in the fourth century A.D.

During this period of decline, the great cities of the Roman Empire fell into disorder. Rich and power-ful Romans, who had once spent most of their time in the cities, retreated to their large estates in the countryside. Free from the cost of maintaining a house in the city, many Roman nobles lavishly deco-rated their rural villas with mosaic artwork.

One of the best examples of this artwork comes from a villa on Sicily, an Italian island in the Mediterra-nean Sea. The estate covers a vast

The design of the Supreme Court Building in Washington, D.C., is based on the ancient writings of the Roman architect Vitruvius.

INSPIRED BY VITRUVIUS

Marcus Vitruvius Pollio, a Roman architect and engineer, wrote the oldest surviving books on architecture. Dating to the first century B.C., Vitruvius's 10-volume work went relatively unnoticed in his lifetime. During the 1400s, however, when Europeans developed a deep interest in the remains of ancient Rome, scholars began to study his writings. Architects of the time regarded Vitruvius's work as an expert guide to classical buildings.

Within his books, Vitruvius described every aspect of ancient Greek and Roman architecture, from the cement mixture needed for mosaic pavements to the designs of arched windows and drainage systems. One of his most important contributions was a description of the styles—called orders—used to decorate classical columns. Classical orders included Doric, Ionic, Corinthian, Composite, and Tuscan, each of which had its own distinctive style. For example, the top, or capital, of a column in the Doric order was very simple. In contrast, the capital of a Corinthian column was highly ornate.

Although Vitruvius's writings are more than 2,000 years old, his work continues to influence modern architects who strive to duplicate the grandeur of ancient buildings. From the Arc de Triomphe in Paris to the Supreme Court Building in Washington, D.C., classical architecture has inspired builders throughout the world.

area, most of which is paved with mosaics. A mosaic portrait indicates that the owner of the home was probably Herculius Maximinus, an official of the Roman Empire in A.D. 300.

One scene shows the lord of the estate arriving home. He is greeted by his servants, who are holding lighted candles. A different section of the same pavement depicts the lord's family enjoying baths in large, heated pools as servants wait on them.

Mosaics in the villa also use the theme of games. A detailed pavement shows chariot races at the Roman circus. The charioteers wear colors representing the four seasons—white for winter, blue for spring, green for summer, and red for fall. The mosaics from the residence of Herculius Maximinus, as well as from other elaborately decorated estates, offer archaeologists a look at the lifestyle of the wealthiest citizens of the late Roman Empire.

A mosaic hunting scene adorns the villa of Herculius Maximinus—an ancient Roman official—on Sicily, an island in the Mediterranean.

MOSAICS OF THE BYZANTINE WORLD

As invaders from northern Europe attacked Rome in the A.D. 300s, the Roman city of Byzantium (modern Istanbul, Turkey) grew in importance. Because Rome had become unsafe, the emperor Constantine made Byzantium the capital of the Roman Empire in A.D. 330. Under Constantine, Byzantium was rebuilt and renamed Constantinople in the emperor's honor.

After Constantine's death in A.D. 337, the empire split into two parts. The Western Roman or Latin Empire, with its capital in Rome, was in the west. Constantinople became the center of the Eastern Roman or Byzantine Empire. As time passed, Rome grew weaker,

and Constantinople grew stronger. Finally, in A.D. 476, northern invaders captured Rome, and the Latin Empire collapsed.

The eastern part, with Constantinople as its capital, survived. This realm thrived for almost a thousand years, producing great music, architecture, and art—including impressive mosaics.

One of the regions in the Byzantine Empire was the Holy Land, a small territory that includes the modern countries of Israel and Jordan. Two religions—Christianity and Judaism—originated in the area. In time, a third religion—Islam—would also take root in the Holy Land. Mosaic pavements decorated many of the churches,

Plants and birds decorate this Byzantine mosaic from the Holy Land—a region that includes the modern countries of Israel and Jordan. Archaeologists discovered the pavement in an ancient Christian church near the Sea of Galilee.

synagogues, and mosques of these religions.

Early Christian Mosaics

The early rulers of the Roman Empire declared Christianity illegal and persecuted the religion's followers. In about A.D. 300, however, Constantine converted to the faith. When he moved the capital of the Roman Empire to Byzantium, he introduced Christianity to members of his government. Eventually, Christianity became the principal religion of the Byzantine Empire.

Early Christians did not allow depictions of people or animals in their artwork. For this reason, Christian churches were originally decorated only with simple geometric patterns.

By the mid-fifth century, these restrictions were lifted, and Christians began using a strict scheme of people and animals to decorate their churches. Artists painted pic-

According to Christian tradition, a mosaicist laid this pavement on the site in northern Israel where Jesus miraculously fed 5,000 people with only five loaves of bread and two fish.

Arab armies invaded the Holy Land in the seventh century and introduced the Islamic religion. Islamic tradition did not allow the depiction of people or animals on artwork. As a result, during Islamic rule, the pieces of many mosaics were rearranged. The tesserae of this picture, which once depicted a lion, were reworked into the image of a plant.

tures of Jesus on domed church ceilings, and images of Mary, the mother of Jesus, decorated arched ceilings behind altars.

Scenes of Jesus' life often appeared in corners below the dome and on the upper sections of church walls. Pictures of various saints and prophets filled the lower sections of the walls. On the floor, a mosaic pavement usually contained scenes of village life.

Archaeologists unearthed one of the oldest Christian pavements in northern Israel. This mosaic shows buildings, trees, plants, and animals. One section depicts two fish and a basket of bread loaves. According to tradition, this mosaic marks the spot where Jesus performed

Archaeologists uncovered this colorful Christian mosaic of a man and his dog in northern Israel.

a famous miracle in which he divided five loaves of bread and two fish among 5,000 people.

In the seventh century, Arab warriors and missionaries introduced the religion of Islam to the peoples of the Middle East. The new faith spread quickly to the Holy Land. In some places, the followers of Islam (called Muslims) took over Christian churches, transforming them into mosques. The traditions of this new religion did not allow artists to depict living beings in their work. As a result, many of the early Christian mosaics that portrayed people and animals were destroyed. Sometimes the pictures were replaced with geometric designs. In other cases, the tesserae were removed, mixed up, and replaced in no apparent order.

GEOMETRIC GENIUSES

During the seventh century A.D., the leaders of Islam—a religion that originated in the Middle East—founded an empire that stretched from Spain in the northwest to India in the southeast. Among Islamic beliefs was the idea that people should not worship images. As a result, laws forbade the depiction of people or animals in public buildings or in mosques (Islamic houses of prayer). Required to work in abstract patterns, Islamic artists created intricate, geometric tilework on the floors and walls of public and religious structures.

Islamic mosaicists made their tiles by pressing clay into thin, square sheets and baking the squares in a kiln, a very hot oven that hardens clay. Artists then applied glaze (a shiny finish) to the tiles or painted the pieces with brightly colored designs.

Attached to flat surfaces with cement, these tiles created dazzling patterns. Artists covered the exteriors of palaces, schools, and mosques. Modern mosaicists continue to adorn Islamic buildings with traditional tilework.

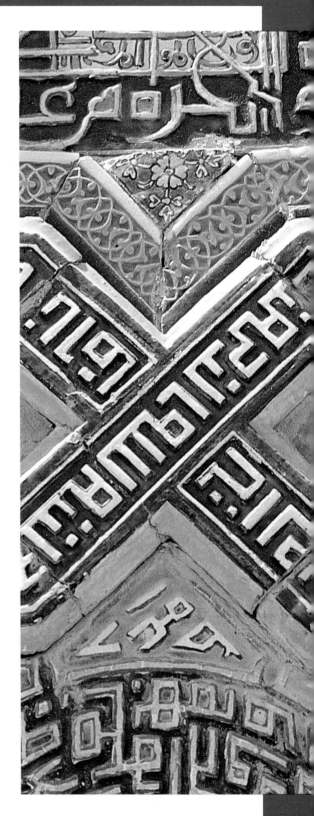

This intricate tilework decorates a monument in Samarkand, Uzbekistan.

Found in Madaba, Jordan, this sixth-century mosaic map depicts the ancient city of Jerusalem. Madaba is famous for its Byzantine mosaics, several of which have been moved to a museum.

Visual Storytelling

The Jews of the Holy Land began crafting mosaics for their synagogues and important buildings during the first century B.C. The earliest of these mosaics were found in the palace of King Herod, who ruled the Holy Land from 73 B.C. to 4 B.C.

Like the early Christians and Muslims, Jews did not allow the depiction of living beings. Scholars believe that by the third century A.D. Jewish rulers had relaxed this policy. This theory is supported by the discovery of a third-century dolphin mosaic among the remains of an important Jewish cemetery.

Under Byzantine rule, which lasted from the fourth century A.D. to the seventh century A.D., the Jews were forbidden to decorate the exteriors of their synagogues. No restrictions, however, applied to synagogue interiors. As a result, many early synagogues in the Holy Land had lavishly ornamented interiors that included mosaic pavements.

The oldest Jewish mosaic of the Byzantine period comes from a

The oldest Jewish mosaic from Byzantine times displays the 12 signs of the zodiac and stands among the ruins of a synagogue in northern Israel *(below).* A view of one small section of the pavement *(left)* shows the artist's great attention to detail.

synagogue near the ancient city of Tiberias in northern Israel. The pavement depicts the 12 signs of the zodiac—constellations of stars visible from the earth.

Byzantine influence can also be seen in a synagogue pavement found in eastern Israel. In this artwork, the seated figure of King David—who ruled Israel in about

Pieced with brightly colored tesserae, this leopard mosaic comes from a Byzantine-era synagogue.

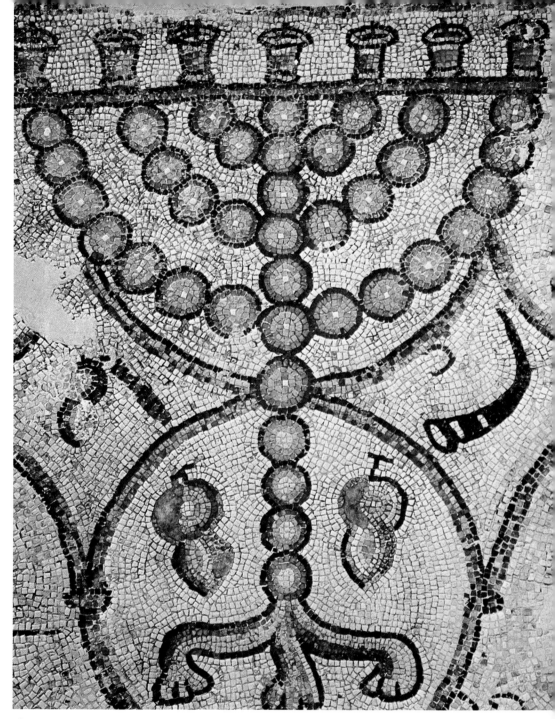

An ancient pavement depicts a menorah, a seven-branched candlestick that is used in Jewish religious services.

1000 B.C.—is shown playing a lyre (harp). Animals have gathered at his feet to listen to the music. Early Jewish mosaicists, who probably did not know how the ancient kings dressed, depicted David in the royal robes of the Byzantine emperors.

Archaeologists believe that Jewish mosaic artists were not as interested in creating great works of art

45

A sixth-century mosaic tells the biblical story of the sacrifice of Isaac, the son of Abraham. As Abraham prepares to kill his son as a tribute to God, an angel replaces Isaac with a ram.

as in telling stories, especially stories from the Bible. For example, one vivid pavement shows pairs of animals entering Noah's Ark at the time of the Great Flood.

Other biblical stories depicted in mosaics include Daniel in the lion's den and Abraham offering to sacrifice his son to God. These mosaics visually transmitted religious stories to villagers, most of whom could not read or write.

Ravenna's Treasures

In A.D. 402, when Rome was no longer safe from invaders, the rulers

A star-studded mosaic *(right)* covers the ceiling of a Christian tomb in Ravenna, Italy. The ceiling frames a mosaic picture of a shepherd *(above)*, which symbolizes God watching over his flock.

of the Western Roman Empire moved their capital to Ravenna, a port city on the eastern coast of the Italian Peninsula. In the sixth century, this part of Italy was conquered by the Byzantine Empire, which brought Ravenna under its rule. During the more than 150 years that the Byzantine governors of Italy lived in Ravenna, the walls and floors of many important buildings were richly decorated with mosaics.

In the sixth century, the people of Ravenna built a church dedicated to Saint Apollinaire, the patron saint of the city. One wall of the church is covered with a mosaic of saints shown on either side of Jesus and Mary. The saints stand in fields of lilies and palm trees. Other walls of the church hold mosaic panels that depict the miracles and the sufferings of Jesus.

The most famous of the Ravenna mosaics decorate the Church of

An apse (domed semicircle) in the Church of St. Apollinaire in Ravenna holds a vivid mosaic of angels guarding a herder and his animals.

Mosaics that portray the Byzantine emperor Justinian (below center) and his wife, Theodora (above), decorate the altar of the Church of St. Vitale in Ravenna.

St. Vitale, which was built a few years after the Church of St. Apollinaire. On one side of the altar, a mosaic panel shows the Byzantine emperor Justinian with members of his royal court. On the other side of the altar stands Justinian's wife, the empress Theodora, with her ladies-in-waiting.

In both works, the figures are set against a gold background, a common feature of Byzantine

Intricate mosaic patterns and pictures adorn the walls and archways of the Mausoleum of Galla Placidia—a Christian tomb in Ravenna.

mosaics. Like saints, Justinian and Theodora are shown with halos around their heads, a sign that they were considered holy.

Constantinople's Mosaics

Byzantine churches in Constantinople were famous for their daz-zling decoration, architecture, and mosaics. Byzantine mosaicists created portraits of Jesus, Mary, the saints, and church leaders, which were often set into solid back-grounds of gold tesserae. Large, elaborate scenes of Jesus' life decorate the upper walls of most churches. Artists did not try to por-tray these pictures realistically or with spatial depth. For this reason, most of the figures appear in somewhat abstract shapes.

During the eighth century, a religious movement known as **iconoclasm** (literally, the practice of image breaking) led to the removal and destruction of many mosaics in Constantinople. Iconoclasts were Christians who believed that people should not worship religious images. While iconoclasm flourished, mosaics containing images of God and people were destroyed. By the ninth century, this movement had died out. Mosaicists again decorated the walls, floors, and ceilings of the great Byzantine churches. The mosaic art form flourished in the

This mosaic depicts the empress Irene, who ruled the Byzantine Empire from 780 to 802. Irene dedicated much of her life to fighting iconoclasm, a religious movement that led to the destruction of many mosaics.

Early Aztec mosaicists decorated this two-headed serpent with turquoise tesserae and added teeth made of white shell.

TURQUOISE AND FEATHERS

The Aztecs flourished in Mexico from the A.D. 1300s to the A.D. 1500s. Aztec artisans decorated weapons, masks, animal figures, and musical instruments with tesserae made of natural stones, bits of shell, and minerals such as turquoise, jade, quartz, obsidian, and gold. Using pitch, a sticky substance made from various plants, the Aztecs attached these materials to wood, stone, leather, or baked clay.

The Aztecs are famous for their bright blue turquoise mosaics, many of which appear on wooden burial masks. Artists also made masks from skulls, decorating them with turquoise tesserae and adding bits of white shell to make teeth and eyes. Some Aztec artists crafted beautiful mosaics out of brightly colored feathers. Intricate feather designs adorned shields, spears, and ceremonial weapons. Although few feather mosaics have survived, those that remain reveal the great skill of the Aztec mosaic artists.

Gold tesserae dominate the walls of Hagia Sophia, a museum in Istanbul, Turkey. Mosaics at the site show scenes of the life of Jesus *(left)* and his mother, Mary *(below)*.

Byzantine world well into the thirteenth century.

The most famous of the Byzantine churches is Hagia Sophia, an enormous building completed in 537 by the emperor Justinian. The walls of Hagia Sophia were intricately decorated with marble and

Inside Hagia Sophia, a decorative arched border surrounds a detailed mosaic of Jesus seated on a throne.

mosaics. For nearly a thousand years, Hagia Sophia—meaning "Holy Wisdom" in Greek—served as a principal church of the Christian faith.

In the fifteenth century, the Ottoman Turks, who followed Islam, conquered the Byzantine Empire. The Turks converted Hagia Sophia into a mosque, covering its great Byzantine mosaics with plaster. The mosaics were preserved, however, and the modern nation of Turkey carefully restored the pictures. In 1935 the country opened Hagia Sophia as a museum where visitors can view the skillful work of the Byzantine mosaicists.

In the sixth century, the emperor Justinian built Hagia Sophia (right) *as an enormous Christian church. The building was converted into an Islamic mosque in the 1400s, when the Ottoman Turks conquered the Byzantine Empire. After restoring the interior* (below), *Turkish officials opened Hagia Sophia as a museum.*

MODERN MOSAICS

This abstract glass mosaic decorates a school in Berlin, Germany.

Present-day artisans continue to make mosaics using the same techniques that ancient craftspeople employed thousands of years ago. Although not as common as they once were, mosaics still decorate the floors, walls, and exteriors of many modern buildings throughout the world.

Modern mosaicists, like their ancient counterparts, use natural, durable materials—such as stone and glass—to make tesserae of many sizes, shapes, colors, and textures. Some mosaicists work for studios that specialize in creating large pavements and wall mosaics. A highly skilled profession, mosaic art requires years of training.

Many artists serve as **apprentices** before taking on their own projects. During this time, the mosaicist-in-training learns how to

Dating to 1905, a brightly colored mosaic from Barcelona, Spain, shows a couple enjoying a summer day *(right)*. A mosaic depicting workers, soldiers, and a family *(above)* stands in the city of Tashkent in Uzbekistan—a former republic of the Soviet Union. Leveled by an earthquake in 1966, Tashkent was rebuilt by workers from other Soviet republics, including Ukraine, whose laborers crafted this mosaic.

An elaborate mosaic (left) adorns the 10-story library of the National Autonomous University of Mexico in Mexico City. A modern mosaicist made uniformly shaped cubes to create a picture of a bridge (below).

shape or select tesserae to create traditional as well as contemporary works. Apprentices also study mortars, glues, and installation techniques. Many modern mosaicists concentrate on learning the skills of restoring ancient mosaics.

Creating large images out of sometimes very tiny tesserae requires time, patience, and skill. This painstaking art form, however, is not only beautiful but also provides us with a durable record of the past. Just as archaeologists study ancient mosaics to learn about early civilizations, future generations may learn about our lives from today's mosaics.

An artist on the Indonesian island of Bali designed this contemporary mosaic using a variety of natural stones.

PRONUNCIATION GUIDE

Antioch (AN-tee-ahk)

Byzantine (BIHZ-uhn-teen)

Constantinople
(kahn-stan-tuh-NOH-puhl)

Hagia Sophia
(HAY-ee-uh so-FEE-uh)

Herculaneum
(her-kyah-LAY-nee-uhm)

Iconoclasm
(eye-KAHN-uh-klaz-uhm)

mosaicist (moh-ZAY-suhst)

mosque (MAHSK)

Olynthus (oh-LIHN-thuhs)

Ostia (AHS-tee-uh)

Pompeii (PAHM-pay)

Ravenna (ruh-VEHN-uh)

Sumer (SOO-muhr)

tesserae (TEHS-uh-ree)

Vitruvius (vuh-TROO-vee-uhs)

Two young artists attach tesserae to a wooden panel. Their work will be mounted next to other small panels to create a colorful wall mosaic.

GLOSSARY

apprentice: a person who learns a trade or artistic technique by working under a skilled craftsperson.

archaeologist: a scientist who studies the material remains of past human life.

cement: a fine, gray powder that contains a variety of minerals, including alumina, lime, magnesia, and silica. When mixed with water and sand, cement becomes a paste that can hold together objects, such as mosaic pieces.

excavator: a person who digs out and removes objects from an archaeological site.

iconoclasm: the practice of destroying artwork that contains religious images. Iconoclasts believe that people should not worship religious images.

pavement: a mosaic set into the floor. Most ancient pavements were made of natural stone, which could bear heavy foot traffic.

pergola: a passageway without a ceiling that is often roofed by a vine-covered trellis.

tesserae: small, colored pieces of stone, glass, tile, or other materials that are used to make mosaic art.

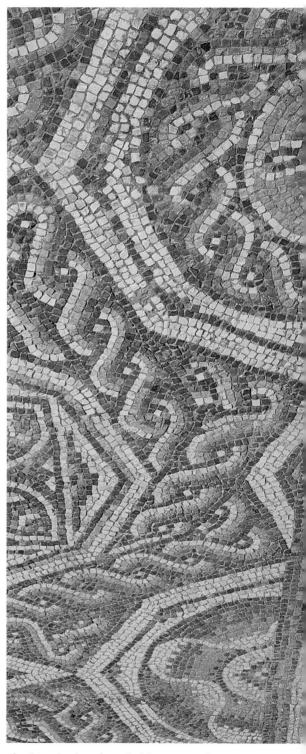

Archaeologists found this geometric mosaic in the North African nation of Tunisia.

INDEX

An artist hand shapes mosaic tiles from clay.

Archaeologists uncovered this ornate mosaic pavement at the ruins of Soloi in northwestern Cyprus.

Photo Acknowledgments

p. 2, © Thomas Ives; pp. 7, 15, 21, 22, 23, 24 (top and bottom), 25, 26, 27, 30, 35, 37, 38, 39, 40, 42, 43 (top and bottom), 44, 45, 46, 47 (top and bottom), 51, 53 (top and bottom), 54, 55 (top and botom), 58 (top), Independent Picture Service; pp. 8, 12, 48, Bob Zehring; pp. 9, 57 (top), 58 (bottom), 59, Betty Groskin; pp. 10 (top and bottom), 11, 14 (top and bottom), 56, Franz Mayer of Munich, Fairfield, NJ; pp. 13, 60, Sue Esbjorson, Courtesy of Laura Schlick/Chrysalis; p. 16, Dale Kakkak/The Circle, Courtesy of Laura Schlick/ Chrysalis; p. 17, Kathy Raskob/IPS, Courtesy of Kristen Cheronis; p. 18, Staatliche Museen, Berlin; p. 19, The Illustrated London News Picture Library; pp. 29 (top and bottom), 31, 33, 56 (bottom), 61, Drs. A. A. M. van der Heyden, Naarden, The Netherlands; pp. 32, p. 49 (top), Minneapolis Public Library and Information Center; p. 34, Library of Congress; p. 41, © Yury Tartarinov; p. 49 (bottom), SCALA/Art Resource; p. 50 Italian Government Travel Office, New York; p. 52, Werner Forman Archive/British Museum, London; p. 62, Elizabeth McDonald; p. 63, Andrew E. Beswick.

Cover photographs: Italian Government Travel Office, New York (front) and Cyprus News Agency (back)

64